The epic adventures of

Mr. FlannelFoot

Smelly Feet

Dear Rollo,

Enjoy the amazing adventures of a very special character-
Mr. FlannelFoot!

Happy Reading!

Vic Gandy

Written by Foz J Foster

Illustrated by Vic Gandy

Written and illustrated at the location of the Great Works Mine near Godolphin Cross in deepest darkest Cornwall, UK

Foz J Foster

Thanks to Jenny Graham for being awesome and lovely.

Appreciation to Barbara Grover from Praa Sands who gave me guidance and her wisdom.

Vic Gandy

Dedicated to my very own mischief makers Rowan & Jack.

Huge thanks to my incredible Husband, Adam for creative support and endless coffee.

Special mention to Emma-leigh Stubbins our 'Manager of Marketing and Mayhem' for incredible ideas and organising the chaos.

And a HUGE thanks to Mr. FlannelFoot of course and the wonderful, amazing and beautiful Cornwall.

And YOU!

CONTENTS

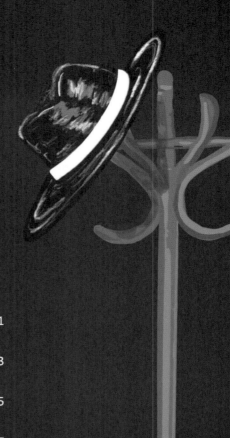

INTRODUCTION

This is the start of the epic adventures of Mr. FlannelFoot. He lives in a world behind mirrors, a mystical world quite different from ours, it's cold, grey and there's not much colour at all there. He doesn't know where he's from, or even how old he is.

There's something very special about Mr. FlannelFoot. He has magical powers, but he can't control them. He moves from his world to ours using mirrors. When he moves into our world, it just happens, and when he's called to our world by unsuspecting parents, his job is to scare children who won't settle down at bedtime into sleeping.

This story was told to me by my grandmother when I was a child when I wouldn't settle down and go to sleep and the story lives on here.

Mr. FlannelFoot has his name because he can move around the house silently because he has flannels neatly wrapped around his feet. He moves from dark areas and shadows very quickly, and children get only a slight glimpse of something moving while they hide in their beds or even under them! But they can't actually see him, only shadows that appear to move.

MR. FLANNELFOOT

dapper,
wide-brim hat
hides eyes

large, green eyes
perfect for
seeing in the
dark

long, black jacket
helps to blend into
the shadows

jacket ripped
from moving through
shards of
mirrors

flannels wrapped
around his feet
for super quiet
creeping

Mr. FlannelFoot's world is called SKROW TAERG, and this is his dark, grey, quiet house in the middle of a forgotten meadow, somewhere else!

Sir piddlebomps

Amy

Bryce

Bryce is six years old, and Amy is eight. They are brother and sister and live with their Mum and Dad, and two fat cats.

They go to the same school and share a bedroom in a small house. They are very active children and play a great deal.

Most of all, they like to stay up late—as late as possible, which is naughty.

Do you like to stay up late?

Mum

Dad

Mr Zipplebum

Mum and Dad are very nice parents and love their children very much.......most of the time.

Mum is a nurse, and Dad works in a warehouse, and they are very tired by the end of the day.

MAC CHEESE AND MONKEYS

Bryce and Amy play a lot during the day, running around and laughing, and as it's the school holidays they have so much spare energy to play, play, and play.

Today they have been to the beach, but they are not tired—not these two little monkeys.

The lazy sun is setting, the light breeze is cooling, and Bryce and Amy have had their favourite meal (mac and cheese), watched some television and taken a bath.

So they get into bed, Dad kisses them "good night" and Mum reads them a story.

It is Saturday night and it's been a long, busy week. Bryce and Amy are wound up like two coiled springs, and Mum and Dad are so tired.

The children are excited about tomorrow's planned picnic and bike ride and sleep is the last thing on their minds.

Mum and Dad take turns going up and down the stairs to get them to sleep. Even the stair carpet is tired of the ups and downs.

Mum stops at the bottom, too tired to step anymore, and calls

"Go to sleep.

Please go to sleep."

But the children just giggle. Mum and Dad look at each other with weary eyes.

"I think it's time for Mr. FlannelFoot,"

says Dad.

BEDTIME STORY

Mum climbs the stairs, holding the rail, pulling herself up, step by step, and swings open the children's bedroom door.

"OK, children. It's time for Mr. FlannelFoot."

Mum sits on the edge of the bed and tells them Mr. FlannelFoot will come and scare them unless they go to sleep. Bryce and Amy listen intently, but still think it's just a story.

"Good Night,"

says Mum, closing the bedroom door and goes downstairs to the sofa.

"I hope that did it,"

says Mum to Dad.

Upstairs, the children still giggle, but they do look around their dark room. It must be just an old story, but what if.........?

12

MONKEYS PLAY

"Let's play I-Spy."

says Amy, turning on the light, and off they go.

13

"I spy, with my little eye, something beginning with S."

says Amy.

Their voices get louder and louder.

"Shadow!"

laughs Bryce.

Downstairs, Mum puts her cocoa down and makes her way to the bottom of the staircase.

"Go to sleep AT ONCE,"

Mum shouts.

14

"Ok, Mum" shouts Amy and Bryce, still inclined to giggle and they carry on with their game.

Mum is so tired, and Dad has fallen asleep on the sofa, no one is watching the television. Mum's mind is racing, thinking of tomorrow's trip and worrying that the children will be overtired and grumpy in the morning.

Slowly, she climbs the stairs once more, and the naughty children quieten down but start to giggle again when she walks into the bathroom.

Mum looks into the bathroom mirror, rubbing her eyes, wearily and calls out,

"Mr. FlannelFoot will visit you."

The children giggle more and Mum, still looking into the mirror, says it again.

"Mr. FlannelFoot will visit you."

Whooooosh! The mirror fogs over as if someone just breathed on it, but Mum knew it wasn't her breath.

Suddenly, at the same time, the house gives a loud CREAK as if it were going to sleep after a busy day, tired of people walking all over it.

The bedroom light goes out!

In the bathroom, Mum smiles into the foggy mirror, for the noisy children are quiet at last.

Meanwhile, the children in their bedroom hear the CREAK too, and it wakes Dad downstairs. The children whisper from under their covers.

"Did you hear that?"

They stop playing their game, and a quietness fills the room. Little did they know that Mr. FlannelFoot had been summoned by Mum saying the magic words twice into a mirror!

They're slightly scared now and from under their covers, they take turns peeking out. Sir Piddlebomps the cat helps too! They all peer out at the shadows in the room with wide-eyed stares.

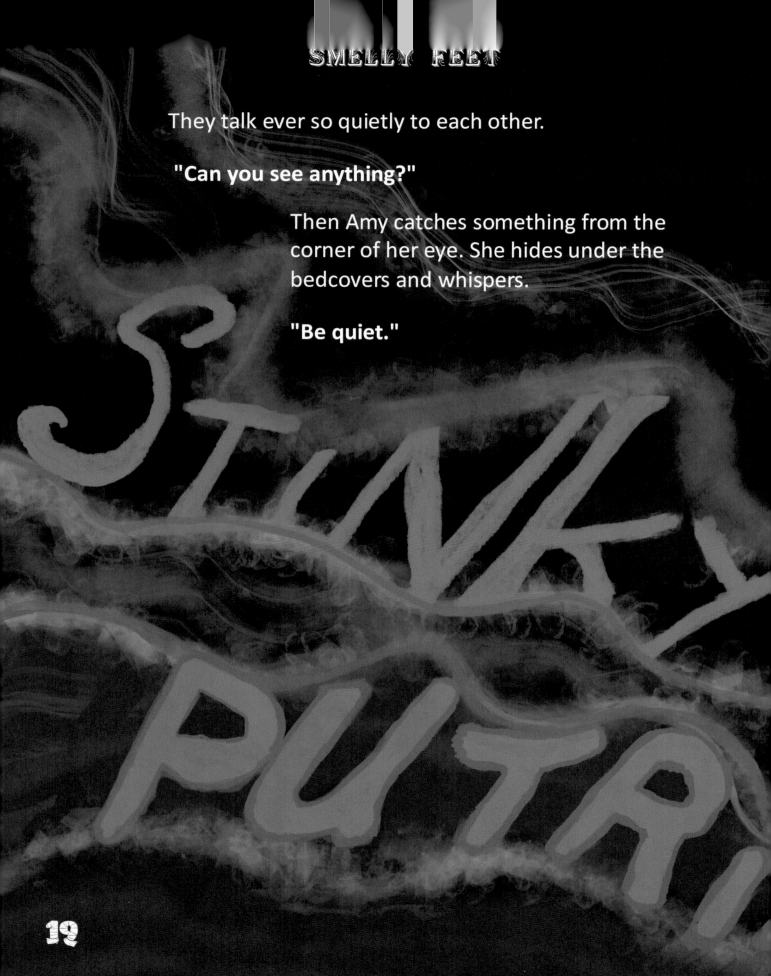

They talk ever so quietly to each other.

"Can you see anything?"

Then Amy catches something from the corner of her eye. She hides under the bedcovers and whispers.

"Be quiet."

Bryce whispers back crossly.

"I am being quiet, but I wish I'd put my socks in the wash basket. They smell like cheesy feet."

Amy is quick to answer.

"You did silly! They are downstairs. You are the smelly one, now be quiet."

In the corner, in the darkest part of the shadowy room, Mr. FlannelFoot smiles and looks down at his flannel-wrapped feet. It's HIS FEET they can smell!

STENCH

WHIFF

PONG

SHADOW DANCING

A little more time goes by and Mr. FlannelFoot
has moved through every shadow in the room.
The children are drowsy now, closing their eyes
they fall to sleep.

Mr. FlannelFoot smiles and disappears back to HIS WORLD, his job done once again.

Something he likes a lot has gone with him... like it always does.

Next morning, at breakfast, Mum and Dad are telling the children about the plans for the day, but the children only want to talk about Mr. FlannelFoot.

 "Is he REAL?"

They ask, again and again.

Mum and Dad grin at each other, and Mum mouths

"It worked!"

23

For the rest of the day, the family has a fantastic time biking and picnicking.

Meanwhile, back in Mr. FlannelFoot's world, he relaxes in his favourite spot, resting his weary feet.

He admires the new addition to his collection...

Days go by and it's another bedtime, and the children will not settle down.

It's Dad's turn to go into their room and repeat the Mr. FlannelFoot story, as it seemed to have worked before.

The children listen intently but need reassurance.

"Dad, it's just a story, isn't it?"

Amy asks nervously.

Dad winks, kisses them, turns out the light, and walks out of the bedroom. Before closing the door, he leans in and looks into their wardrobe mirror, reflecting the children and says........

"Don't forget Mr. FlannelFoot will visit you!"

For some strange reason, he says it again.

"Don't forget Mr. FlannelFoot will visit you!"

The house gives a loud **CREEAAKK**

As Dad notices the mirror has fogged over, the children cry out in alarm.

"WHAT WAS THAT?"

"It's all right, just the house going to sleep like you two."

Dad says as he closes the door.

Out on the landing Dad thinks to himself about the cheesy smell in the bedroom. Is it the children's laundry?

Downstairs, Dad goes
checking every floor
board and every stair
for a loose joint, but
there are no creaks.

"It's funny," he says to Mum.

"The house creaked again. It never did that before."

"It must have." says Mum

30

Mr. FlannelFoot is summoned again, but this time by accident. He has moved again from his world and he knows he can't be seen. He lurks in the shadows behind the brightly coloured curtains in the children's room.

It is very quiet as Amy and Bryce are hiding under the covers, so he decides to move about as it's boring just standing there. He looks under the brim of his hat and moves to another corner, ever so quickly, faster than a blink of an eye and silently of course, because of the flannels on his feet.

Both children catch a glimpse of a shadow and are now scared, but Mr. FlannelFoot is smiling as he sees a vivid sock hanging from Amy's bed. Ah! He likes this one.

Bryce and Amy have stretched their covers over their heads so tightly that their noses poke out. Mr. FlannelFoot waits for the children to move and it is Amy, the inquisitive one, who peeps out, her eyes like full moons.

 "It's so dark in here, Bryce, and your feet STINK," Amy says.

Mr. FlannelFoot grins. His feet are the stinky ones. He moves to a gap between the wardrobe and wall, he notices the mirror fogged over, and with his long finger he writes **"night, night."**

Amy glimpses SOMETHING and bolts under the covers so quickly that it is a world record for bolting, if there is such a thing. As Amy and Bryce fall asleep, Mr. FlannelFoot is very pleased with himself. He chuckles and disappears back to his world with another addition.

There is another thing you need to know about Mr. FlannelFoot. He likes colourful socks. He cannot wear any as he has flannels on his feet, so when he leaves a bedroom to go back to his world, he takes just ONE sock.

Have you ever noticed one sock is always missing on wash days?

SATISFACTION

More days go by and the children have been really good, so no visits from Mr. FlannelFoot. Dad is washing the clothes, and both children are playing in the kitchen.

"Dad!" shouts Amy.

"That was so fun when you wrote on the wardrobe mirror the other night."

Dad is confused.

"Glad you liked it..."

He says, glancing at Mum, who shrugs, and neither of them understand. Mum carries on folding the clothes and putting the clean socks into pairs. Two odd socks are missing, so she checks the dryer, but there is nothing there. She asks Dad,

"Honey, have you seen two spare brightly coloured socks anywhere?"

Dad and the children check everywhere, but the socks are nowhere to be found.

Meanwhile, Mr. FlannelFoot is relaxing in his house, looking proudly at his two new treasures, his work done again, waiting for his next adventure.

What's that smell of
cheese in the air?

Mr. FlannelFoot is
standing there.

He can glide through
doors and locks, but all
he wants is bright new
socks.

So close your eyes and
don't dare peep.

And he will go - if you're
ASLEEP

Look out for the next book in the series "The Sleepover"

WANTED

Looter, Lurker
and
Mischief-Maker

Use a phone and take a pic of your masterpiece and send it to
submit@mrflannelfoot.co.uk

Question 1

What's the name of one of the cats in this story?

(A)   Mr. Wigglesworth

(B)   Mrs Moonbuggy

(C)   Sir Piddlebomps

(D)   Zodiacmindwarp

Question 2

On page 7 what does Amy do with the lights?

(A)   Cover them

(B)   Close her eyes

(C)   Turn them off

(D)   Turn them on

Question 3

What's the name of the second book in the Mr. FlannelFoot series?

(A)   The sleepover

(B)   Meets Santa Claus

(C)   Saves the day

(D)   Meets a Mermaid

Question 4

What fogged over when Mr. FlannelFoot enters the house?

(A)   A window

(B)   Wardrobe door

(C)   A mirror

(D)   A toy

ANSWERS

Question 1

(C) Sir Piddlebomps

Question 2

(D) Turn them on

Question 3

(A) The Sleepover

Question 4

(C) A mirror

Whatever your score Mr. FlannelFoot says **"well done indeed"**

Ready for another quiz? Use the QR code or go to
https://www.mrflannelfoot.co.uk/quiz-smelly-feet

GREATWORKS STUDIOS

 @greatworksstudios

 @greatworks_studios

 @mrflannelfoot

 @FosterFozJ

 www.mrflannelfoot.co.uk

"A world without all your socks in their pairs is chaos."

Mr. FlannelFoot

Printed in Great Britain
by Amazon